This book is dedicated to
our beautiful Beth. Welcome to the family.
And to a special school in Spain
where I met my future editor, Aileen,
and Natalie's papa, Antonio.

Edited by Aileen Andres Sox
Designed by Dennis Ferree
Art by Mary Rumford
Typeset in 18/26 Windsor

ISBN: 0-8163-1233-8

94 95 96 97 98 • 5 4 3 2 1

Baby in the Laundry Basket

A Christmas Story

By Linda Porter Carlyle

Illustrated by Mary Rumford

Pacific Press Publishing Association
Boise, Idaho
Oshawa, Ontario, Canada

What *is* a manger?" asked Natalie, frowning. "Why did Mary put Jesus in one?"

Mama looked up from the book she was reading aloud. "Well," she said, "it's a kind of box that animals eat from."

"You mean like a *dog dish*?" Natalie asked, her eyes very wide.

Mama laughed. "No. Not exactly like a dog dish. A manger would be bigger. A manger holds hay for bigger animals to eat. Like donkeys," she said. "Hay for the donkeys to eat would smell fresh and sweet and be soft to lie on."

"Was Mary sad because she had to put Baby Jesus in a manger to sleep?" asked Natalie.

"Oh, I don't think so," said Mama. "She was probably glad there was nice soft hay there for Him to sleep on. Lots of people in this world have slept on hay. It's soft, and it's warm. It would make a perfect baby bed.

ut I don't think Jesus had to sleep in the manger for very long," she continued. "I'm sure Joseph found a house for his family as soon as he could. And since he was a carpenter, he probably made a beautiful bed for Jesus."

Natalie peeked into the laundry basket on the floor beside her. "This basket makes a perfect baby bed too," she said. "The towels are soft and warm. And it's just the right size. When will he wake up so I can feed him?"

Mama got up and looked into the laundry basket. "I don't know," she said. "You never know with babies. Come on in the kitchen, and we'll fix some formula so it will be ready when he does wake up."

Natalie sat on the couch. She held baby Adam close to her tummy. She held the baby bottle at just the right angle. Baby Adam sucked and sucked. He looked at Natalie with his dark, dark, brown eyes. "I want to keep this baby, Mama," Natalie said.

Mama smiled. "We can keep him only until tomorrow when his daddy comes to pick him up. We can keep him and take care of him only for a little while. He came to stay with us only because his mama is sick in the hospital, and his daddy had to work."

I love this baby," whispered Natalie, softly.

"That's the way mommies and daddies feel," said Mama. "Baby Adam is the best and most perfect gift that God could give his parents."

atalie looked at Mama. "Am I your best and
most perfect gift?" she asked.

"You certainly are!" answered Mama.

"Did I come all wrapped up in pretty paper with a bow on?" asked Natalie with a grin.

"Nope." Mama laughed. "No bows. Not even in your hair."

C an we put the laundry basket on the floor by my bed?" asked Natalie.

"Sure," said Mama. "I can hear him in there if he wakes up and fusses." She picked up the basket with

baby Adam inside and carried it into Natalie's bed-
room. She sat down on the side of Natalie's bed. "You
know," Mama said, "every time I see a new baby, I
think of the best and most perfect gift of all. Do you
know what that was?"

atalie sat up in bed and hugged her knees. She thought for a minute. "I know!" she exclaimed. "Baby Jesus!"

"You're right!" said Mama. "Jesus gave Himself to the whole world. He is everybody's best and most perfect gift."

Natalie and Mama stood on the front porch. They watched baby Adam's daddy put him into his car seat.

"Thank you for taking such good care of him!" baby Adam's daddy called.

Natalie and Mama waved goodbye. They watched the car drive away.

Inside the house, the laundry basket looked empty and lonely. "I wish I could have given baby Adam a Christmas present," Natalie said sadly.

"But you did!" said Mama.

Natalie looked at Mama.

"You took such good care of him. You fed him and held him and loved him when he was here. Loving someone is the best and most perfect gift we can give them."

Natalie sat on the floor and looked at the twinkling lights on the Christmas tree. She looked at the pile of presents under the tree. She thought about the best and most perfect gifts—the ones that couldn't be wrapped up in paper with pretty bows on top. "I love you, Mama," she called.

"I love you too," Mama called back from the kitchen.

Natalie smiled. "I love You, Jesus," she whispered. She listened. She could almost hear Jesus saying, "I love you too!"